AF584817

This book belongs to

Empowered MOO

Special words for little people

by Davina Rankin

First published in 2020 by Davina Rankin

www.ohmymoo.com.au

ISBN 9781761282232 (print)

Published in Australia and New Zealand by:

Booktopia Publishing, a division of Booktopia Group Ltd
Unit E1, 3-29 Birnie Avenue, Lidcombe, NSW 2141, Australia

Illustrations by Tanya Maneki, @tanya.maneki

Printed and bound in China by Reliance Printing (Shenzhen) Co. Ltd

briobooks.com.au

For my little darling, Mila-Mae

I am

SPECIAL

I am

KIND

I am
FEARLESS

KAPOW!
BOOM!

I am
BEAUTIFUL

I am WORTHY OF BLESSINGS

Gifts from
the universe

I am
DESERVING
OF LOVE

I can do
ANYTHING
I put
MY MIND TO

I can be

ANYTHING

I want

TO BE

YogaMoo
NurseMoo
PoliceMOO
ArtistMOO

I can MAKE A DIFFERENCE